GIRLS SURVIVE

Girls Survive is published by Stone Arch Books
A Capstone Imprint
1710 Roe Crest Drive
North Mankato, Minnesota 56003
www.capstonepub.com

Library of Congress Cataloging-in-Publication Data
Names: Gunderson, Jessica, author. | Forsyth, Matt, illustrator. | Trunfio, Alessia, 1990– artist.
Title: Carrie and the Great Storm : a Galveston Hurricane survival story / by Jessica Gunderson ; illustrated by Matt Forsyth ; cover illustration by Alessia Trunfio.
Other titles: Girls survive.
Description: North Mankato, Minnesota : Stone Arch Books, [2019] | Series: Girls survive | Summary: In early September 1900, twelve-year-old Carrie of Galveston is looking forward to spending Saturday night at her friend's house, until her parents are invited to a very important party. Carrie is forced to stay home and take care of her little brother, but a boring chore turns into a nightmare when the storm surge from the Great Hurricane hits and their house is swept off its foundation. Carrie must think quickly and not panic if she is going to keep herself and her brother alive.
Identifiers: LCCN 2019003239 | ISBN 9781496583857 (hardcover) | ISBN 9781496584472 (pbk.) | ISBN 9781496583901 (ebook pdf)
Subjects: LCSH: Hurricanes—Texas—Galveston—History—20th century—Juvenile fiction. | Floods—Texas—Galveston—History—20th century—Juvenile fiction. | Survival—Texas—Galveston—History—20th century—Juvenile fiction. | Brothers and sisters—Juvenile fiction. | Galveston (Tex.)—History—20th century—Juvenile fiction. | CYAC: Hurricanes—Fiction. | Floods—Fiction. | Survival—Fiction. | Brothers and sisters—Fiction. | Galveston (Tex.)—History—20th century—Fiction. | LCGFT: Historical fiction.
Classification: LCC PZ7.G963 Car 2019 | DDC 813.6 [Fic]—dc23
LC record available at https://lccn.loc.gov/2019003239

Designer:
Charmaine Whitman

Cover art:
Alessia Trunfio

Image credits:
Anda Marie Photography, 112; Library of Congress, 105 (bottom);
Shutterstock: Everett Historical, 105 (top), kaokiemonkey (pattern), back cover and throughout, Max Lashcheuski (background), 2 and throughout

Printed and bound in the USA.
PA70

CARRIE
AND THE GREAT STORM

A Galveston Hurricane Survival Story

by Jessica Gunderson

illustrated by Matt Forsyth

STONE ARCH BOOKS
a capstone imprint

CHAPTER ONE

I wanted rain. The entire city of Galveston, Texas, wanted rain. The air was so hot and sticky it hurt to breathe.

"I feel like I'm going to melt in this heat!" my best friend, Betsy, exclaimed. We were trudging home from school through the thick heat along Galveston's busy Broadway Street. Streetcars rattled past. Sweaty horses clopped by, pulling carriages.

Betsy paused and wiped away a dark curl that clung to her forehead. I stopped too, adjusting my straw hat. "Hopefully tomorrow is cooler,"

I said as we continued across the street toward our neighborhood.

Even the heat couldn't keep down my excitement for the weekend. I had just turned twelve, our first week of school was over, and I was going to spend Saturday night at Betsy's house. And the best part was that Anna, Betsy's sixteen-year-old sister, was home from boarding school in Houston for the weekend.

I loved Anna. She was beautiful and funny. Betsy and I had been friends since we were three years old. Anna was like the big sister I'd never had. I'd always wanted a sister. Instead, I had an annoying six-year-old brother named Henry. He certainly couldn't braid my hair like Anna did. Or take me shopping for just the right shoes to go with a dress.

"I'm going to wear my best dress tomorrow," I said dreamily. I gazed at the well-dressed women walking past. One young woman in a violet dress stood looking in a shop window. I paused, staring at her.

"Look at her hair!" I whispered to Betsy. "She has the new pompadour style. Do you think Anna—"

"Look out!" Betsy exclaimed. She yanked me onto the sidewalk just as a horse-drawn carriage galloped past. I hadn't even realized I'd drifted into the street.

"Carrie Mills! You could have been killed!" Betsy said, still gripping my arm. "What would I do without my best friend?"

My heart was clattering as fast as the horses' hooves. "He would have slowed down," I said, trying to convince her—and myself. I swallowed. "Anyway, do you think Anna could do my hair in a pompadour?"

"Maybe," Betsy said. "She loves to do hair. And she loves you." Betsy wrinkled her nose. She didn't love her sister like I did.

"What do you think of our new teacher, Miss Stapleton?" Betsy asked, changing the subject.

"She's nice," I replied. "But she's much too young to be dressed so drably. Honestly, she's worn the same dress all week, just in different shades of gray."

Betsy laughed. "You are always so concerned about clothes and hair," she said.

She was right. I did spend a lot of time thinking about clothes, dreaming about styles I would wear when I was older. Sometimes I even drew my own designs on scraps of paper.

"I think Miss Stapleton is smart," Betsy went on. "She speaks her mind. And she doesn't care what anyone thinks. I want to be like her someday."

"I want to be like Anna someday," I said.

Betsy rolled her eyes. "Sometimes I think you like Anna more than you like me."

"That's not true!" I protested. Then I gave her a teasing grin. "Well, maybe a little."

"You're incorrigible," Betsy said.

"Incorrigible?" I repeated. Betsy was always using big words. She was smart—maybe even smarter than Miss Stapleton.

"It means 'unruly.' Like my hair in this heat!" Betsy tugged at her hair again.

"Hopefully this humidity breaks," I said. "Otherwise our pompadours will never stay up!"

"My dad says a storm is coming," Betsy said. "Maybe that will cool us off a bit."

I groaned. "Another storm."

Galveston always had so many storms. The city was on an island just off the coast of Texas. Tropical storms often built up over the Gulf of Mexico and crashed onto the island.

Sometimes the Gulf would rise so much the streets flooded. The storms could be loud and scary, but they always passed quickly. It never took long for things to go back to normal.

Even though I didn't like storms, I loved Galveston. I knew it could weather any storm. It was one of the fastest-growing cities in the United States. Some people called it the "New York of the Southwest."

My mother was obsessed with Galveston's growing social scene. Nearly every weekend, she and my father went to musicals at the Grand Opera House. They also attended parties and balls hosted by the city's richest families. We weren't rich, but my mother liked to pretend otherwise.

Whenever they got home from an event, she would tell me all about who was there. I loved to hear her describe the latest fashions the ladies were wearing. I wanted to be a designer myself someday, although I hadn't told anyone that.

We reached the corner where Betsy would turn to go to her house on Avenue O and I would continue to mine on Avenue Q. A hot, sudden gust of wind whipped at my dress.

"Here comes that storm," Betsy said, hugging me goodbye. "I'll see you tomorrow!"

I skipped the rest of the way home, dreaming of Anna and pompadours and late-night whispers with Betsy. Tomorrow. It would be the best day ever.

The Mills's house
Friday, September 7, 1900
3:30 p.m.

I stepped inside the house, feeling relief from the scorching sun. The dark coolness of the house made me realize just how hot it was outside. The storm sure would be welcome. My legs felt wet with sweat under my petticoats. Having to wear all these layers sometimes made me wish I could dress like my little brother, Henry, who could zoom around in short knickers.

As if he'd heard me thinking about him, Henry poked his head around the corner. He gave a shy giggle and ducked out of sight again. He was always sweet and playful the first time he saw me each day. I liked that side of him. But in no time, he'd be loud and demanding. I sighed.

"There you are, Carrie!" my mother called from the top of the stairs. She glided down the steps, fanning herself with an envelope in her hand. She held the envelope out to me. "Look at this!"

"Mama's been invited to a party!" Henry squealed, reappearing. He barreled toward Mama and buried his head in her skirt.

I took the envelope. Before I even had a chance to read the invitation, my mother said,

"Can you believe it? Your father and I have been invited to the Gilberts' party. It's the event of the season!"

I scanned the invitation. "But it's tomorrow afternoon," I said.

"Yes, tomorrow." My mother nodded. "I don't have much time to prepare. I need you to help me choose a dress. Nothing too fancy, but something elegant that will help me stand out. All the highest society members will be there . . ."

"While they're at the party, you can teach me how to play solitaire!" Henry shouted. He jumped up and down so hard that the whole house seemed to shake.

"I won't be here," I told him. "I'll be at Betsy's house."

"Oh!" My mother's smile dropped. "I'm sorry, Carrie. But you'll need to stay home and watch Henry tomorrow."

My face grew as hot as the Galveston sun. "No!" I said. "You promised!" I'd been looking forward to my first sleepover for weeks.

My mother shrugged. "You'll have more chances to stay at Betsy's. I'll never have another chance to attend this party. Now, come and help me—"

I whirled past her and rushed up the stairs. Tears blinded my sight. I ran into my room and flopped down on the bed, my mind racing. Then I thought of Papa. Papa almost always gave in to me. I would convince him to let me go. I had to.

I heard the front door open. Papa's boots smacked the floor. He was home. This was my chance.

CHAPTER TWO

"No," Papa said. He sat down at the dining room table and took off his hat. "This party is important to your mother. You'll need to stay home and watch Henry."

"Surely someone else can stay with him," I pleaded. "What about Mrs. Whitaker?" Our part-time housekeeper was as good a solution as any.

"Saturday is her day off. 'No' is my final answer." He closed his eyes and rubbed his temples.

I'd never seen Papa so stern. He seemed worried about something, something that had nothing to do with me or the party.

"What's wrong, Papa?" I asked. "Was it a hard day at the bank?" Papa worked at Galveston City Bank, investing money for some of Galveston's wealthiest residents.

But Papa shook his head. "Work was fine. It's just . . . have you ever felt as if someone isn't telling you the whole story?" he said. "That's how I've been feeling about this storm. The Weather Bureau is saying it's a tropical storm, not a hurricane, and that it'll likely miss us. But feel this air!" He held up a finger. "It's so still and ominous."

I loved when Papa spoke to me like an adult. Most other grown-ups still treated me like a child. "Don't worry, Papa. We've had tropical storms before."

"The Weather Bureau raised the red storm-warning flag today," Papa went on. "That's the least they could do."

"I wonder if the Gilberts know about the warning flag," I said. "Maybe the party will be canceled!" I gave him a hopeful look.

Papa looked at me and shook his head. "Oh, Carrie. Sometimes we need to think about something other than ourselves."

Just then a knock sounded at the front door. I was happy for the interruption. I didn't want to answer Papa's words or even think about what he had said. My mother was the one being selfish—not me.

I hurried to the hall and swung the door open. I was nearly knocked over by Anna. She hugged me and pulled me out the doorway. Over her shoulder I spotted Betsy standing at the bottom of our front steps.

"Carrie!" Anna squealed. "Come look at the waves with us!"

I hugged Anna back and grinned at Betsy. "What waves?" I asked.

"Practically the whole city is at the Gulf bcach," Anna told me. "The waves are so high! Higher than you've ever seen!"

"Let me see if I can go," I said. I went back inside and approached my father, who was still sitting at the dining room table. "Papa, can I go to the beach with Betsy and Anna?" I asked.

He nodded. "But take Henry with you."

I sighed. Why did Henry always have to tag along? I was about to protest, but just then Henry came into the room and climbed into Papa's lap. I looked at my little brother's pleading eyes. He'd clearly overheard our conversation.

"All right," I said. "Come on, Henry. We're going to the beach."

He slid off Papa's lap. "Are we going swimming?" he cried.

"Just splashing about in the waves," I said. "Now hurry up and put your shoes on."

Henry did as he was told, and together we headed outside. He skipped in front of Betsy, Anna, and me as we made our way to the Gulf beach, just a few blocks away.

As we sauntered down the sidewalk, we came across a group of black kids. They moved to the other side to let us pass. The kids were about our age, but I didn't know any of them. Galveston was segregated, so we went to separate schools.

"I'm so happy to be home for the weekend," Anna said as we walked. "I have so much to tell you about boarding school. My favorite class is ballroom dancing. I've learned some new dances to teach you tomorrow!"

I swallowed. "I have something to tell you both," I said. "I can't come over tomorrow."

Betsy gasped. "Why not?"

"My parents were invited to the Gilberts' party. And I have to stay home with Henry." I glared at my brother's back as he darted along the sidewalk in front of us.

"But we've been planning this for weeks!" Betsy exclaimed. "Mama is making your favorite pie."

"And I wanted to try out new hairstyles on you!" Anna said. "Your hair is perfect for a new braid I learned."

"I know," I said quietly. I felt close to tears again.

Anna put her hand on my shoulder. She seemed to sense how upset I was. "It's OK, Carrie. I'll be back again for the holidays."

"But that's December!" I said. "Three months away!"

"Time will go fast," Anna promised. "Now, let me tell you about the girls I met at boarding school."

As Anna chattered away, I fanned my face with my hand. It was hot—even hotter than earlier. Only a few small clouds drifted in the sky. Even the gusts of wind felt like fiery dragon's breath.

"My father says a storm is coming," I told the girls. I blinked against the bright sun. "It's hard to believe. There are hardly any clouds."

"He's right," Betsy said. "The barometer is falling."

"The what?" Anna asked with a giggle. She nudged me, and I giggled too, shrugging. We both knew we'd never be as smart as Betsy.

"Barometer. It's an instrument that determines the pressure of the atmosphere. It falls when a storm is coming and rises for good weather," Betsy explained. She gave me a look. "Miss Stapleton talked about it in school today."

"I must have been daydreaming," I admitted.

As we neared the beach, the sound of the waves drowned out any further conversation. They were larger than I'd ever seen, rising high, curling, and crashing onto the sand in a white froth. Water was covering most of the beach, and on the horizon, swells rose like dark mountains against the sky.

What Anna had said on the porch was true—it looked as if the entire city of Galveston was here. Bicyclists rode up and down the beach. Children splashed in the waves. I saw the group of kids we'd passed. They stayed on the other side of the beach. Even outside of our separate schools, black kids and white kids didn't mingle.

"Can I go wading?" Henry asked.

"Sure," I said. "But stay close." I helped him take off his shoes, and he darted down the beach, stopping every once in a while to pick up seashells.

"Hello, girls!" called a voice.

I turned and saw Miss Stapleton riding toward us on her bicycle. She stopped and gestured out at the Gulf.

"Isn't it amazing?" she said.

"We were just talking about you," I told our teacher. "And what you said about the barometer falling."

Miss Stapleton smiled at me. "I'm glad you were listening," she said.

I didn't look at Betsy, but I knew her eyes were rolling.

"Look how dark the swells are," Miss Stapleton said. "When storms are really strong, they can pick up sand from the bottom of the ocean. The sand swirls around in the waves. That's what makes them so dark."

"My father thinks the storm will be worse than the Weather Bureau says," I told her.

Miss Stapleton nodded. "Storms are hard to predict. The storm could change direction. It might not even land in Galveston."

Anna suddenly clutched my arm. "Carrie. Where's Henry?"

I scanned the beach. Henry was nowhere to be seen. I took off down the beach, my feet sinking in the wet sand. "Henry?" I called. "Henry!"

My call was carried away by the roar of the sea. A wave curled at my feet, leaving behind dark sand and white bubbles as it slunk away.

Where is Henry? I thought in a panic.

I scanned the beach again and saw a group of children tossing a ball. He had to be with them. He just had to.

I ran toward the children. The group broke apart fearfully when they saw me barreling toward them at full speed. "Have you seen my little brother?" I gasped. "He's wearing knickers and a white shirt.

He has a lot of freckles and . . ." I trailed off as the children shook their heads no.

Then I saw him. My brother was skipping along the shore, close to the water. And right behind him, a giant wave, open like a mouth, was barreling toward shore, ready to swallow Henry whole.

CHAPTER THREE

"Henry!" I screamed. I scooped him up, just as the towering wave toppled over us.

The water clutched at my skirt, trying to drag us out to sea. I held Henry tight, digging my feet into the sand. Eventually the wave receded, leaving us both drenched.

Henry wriggled from my arms. "I'm wet, Carrie! And so are you," he said gleefully. "This is fun!"

I grabbed his arm and pulled him toward the street. "You shouldn't have gone so close to the water," I said. "I told you to stay close! You could have drowned!" But even as I was scolding him, I was also scolding myself. I shouldn't have let Henry run off alone. I should have been watching him.

Seawater squished inside my shoes, and my wet skirt bogged me down as we made our way back toward Anna, Betsy, and Miss Stapleton. They were all watching us with a combination of concern and relief.

"I'm so glad you found him," Betsy said.

"One thing I've learned as a teacher is that you can't take your eyes off children, even for a second," Miss Stapleton said as she mounted her bicycle. "Or else mischief and danger will ensue."

I smiled and shrugged, trying to act nonchalant, even though terror still whipped at my insides. "I'm soaked," I said. "But at least I'm not so hot anymore."

Miss Stapleton rode away, and I looked back at the Gulf. Clouds now loomed in the distance, shutting out the setting sun. The beach, which had seemed fun and exciting at first, was now dark and menacing. A small part of me wanted to stay with Anna and Betsy, but mostly I just wanted to go home.

I turned to Henry. "Put on your shoes," I said. "Let's go."

He stuffed his feet into his shoes, and I gave Betsy and Anna hugs goodbye. I clutched Henry's hand firmly in mine as we walked toward the street. I looked back at Betsy and Anna to give them a final wave, but they didn't see me. They stood arm in arm, facing the hazy setting sun and watching the crashing waves.

The Mills's house
Saturday, September 8, 1900
7:00 a.m.

In the morning, I woke to rain pounding against the windowpanes. The storm had arrived. I tugged my sheets up to my chin and closed my eyes.

A soft knock sounded at the door.

"Time for breakfast," Mama called through the door.

"Just a few more minutes," I said. I felt exhausted from the first week of school and the episode at the beach. All night long my dreams had been peppered with Anna, Betsy, and Henry, their faces floating in and out. When they opened their mouths to speak, all I could hear was the roar of the sea.

Finally, I climbed out of bed, got dressed, and went downstairs. Papa was sitting at his usual spot at the dining room table. His breakfast was untouched, and he was staring down at the newspaper in front of him. I saw the headline of a small story, "Storm in the Gulf."

Mama sat across from him, daintily eating her biscuit. She looked up when I entered. "Hurry and eat. You need to help me find a dress to wear for this afternoon," she said. "You were supposed to do it yesterday," she added sharply.

"I was watching Henry," I countered.

Papa looked toward the window. "I can't believe this party is still going to happen today."

"The Gilberts would never cancel their party," Mama said, looking horrified. "It's a yearly tradition. And we're finally invited!"

I suddenly realized how important the event was to my mother and felt bad for being so angry at her yesterday. Papa was right—I shouldn't think only about myself. I could sleep over at Betsy's anytime. The Gilberts' party only happened once a year.

"I'm sure it won't be canceled, Mama," I assured her.

Mama gave me a small smile. "When you're done eating," she said more gently, "come up to my room."

"This one? Or maybe this one?" I said, holding out two dresses, one blue with a high collar, the other mauve with a buttoned jacket.

I loved going through Mama's wardrobe. She always ordered the latest fashions from the Sears, Roebuck catalog.

"The blue one," Mama said. "The one with the feathered hat."

"You might want the matching umbrella too," I suggested, holding out the blue silk parasol. "It doesn't look like the rain will let up by this afternoon."

"The weather always ruins everything," Mama said. "There was to be afternoon tea in the Gilberts' garden. Oh, how I wanted to see their garden! It's the grandest one on Broadway. Now the party will be moved inside, I suppose."

I paged through Mama's fashion magazines as she talked about who would be at the party, what they would be wearing, and what she might talk about. Mama was always concerned with what people thought of her. I remembered what Betsy had said earlier about Miss Stapleton—that she didn't care what anyone thought. Miss Stapleton and my mother were definitely opposites.

"Will the mayor be there?" I asked, turning the page.

I didn't listen to Mama's answer. I was too focused on what I saw: a beautiful, gold-colored chiffon dress with balloon sleeves that tapered at the wrist. The designer's name, printed at the bottom of the picture, was female. I knew women could be dressmakers, but I had no idea women could actually design clothing.

What would it be like to have my name printed in a magazine? I wondered.

"Carrie, stop daydreaming," Mama said, almost as if she could hear my thoughts. I snapped to attention. "Which broach? The ruby or the gold?"

Saturday, September 8, 1900
1:00 p.m.

The rain was still coming down hard when it was time for my parents to leave for the party. Papa went out to pull the horse and carriage to the yard, close to the door so my mother wouldn't get wet. I waited with my mother near the front windows, and we watched the rain zigzag from the sky. The front yard looked like one giant puddle.

Just then Papa pulled into the yard. He leapt up the steps and opened the door for Mama. He held his jacket over her head, and together they rushed to the carriage.

A gust of wind sent a smattering of rain pellets against the windowpane, and I lost sight of my parents. A sudden panic seized me. "Wait! Don't go!" I cried, shoving my face against the pane.

But they couldn't hear me. The horse splashed its hooves in the water, the carriage lurched forward, and then they were gone.

I shook off my feeling of dread. *It's just another storm,* I told myself. *It will be over soon.*

My thoughts turned to Betsy. What were she and Anna doing right now? I pictured them in Anna's room, Anna showing Betsy how to ballroom dance. Oh, how I wished I could be there!

"Let's play!" Henry shrieked. A ball bounced off my shoulder and rolled to the floor.

"Henry!" I scolded. "No playing ball in the house."

"But I can't play with it outside," he whined. "It's raining."

"Then find something else to do!" I snapped. I ran up to my room, slamming the door behind me. I didn't want to play with Henry. All I wanted was to be with Anna and Betsy.

I lay on my bed, staring at the ceiling. Wind pounded at the windows, and Henry pounded at my door. I ignored both sounds, thinking only about how miserable I was.

It's not fair that I'm stuck at home while everyone else is doing something fun, I thought angrily.

Just then my door opened a crack, and Henry's face appeared. "Carrie?" he whimpered. "Look outside. The storm is getting worse."

I sighed, annoyed by the interruption, and sat up. I'd been through storms before. How bad could it be? But when I peered through my curtains my heart stopped a beat, then pounded as fast as the rain. Our street now looked like a river, flowing quickly and angrily. A chair bobbed past. As I watched, a tree branch snapped, whipped through the air, and slammed against the house across the street.

I couldn't believe what I was seeing. The water had never risen this high before. And where on earth had that chair come from? When had the storm gotten so bad? And what was I going to do?

CHAPTER FOUR

The Mills's house
Saturday, September 8, 1900
3:00 p.m.

Henry flung himself onto my bed. "I'm scared!" he whispered. And then he started to cry. A gust of wind shook the windowpane, and Henry wailed even louder.

I was scared too, but I couldn't show it. "Don't worry, Henry," I said. "It's just overflow. It happens all the time in Galveston! Remember last year?"

Henry wiped his eyes. "I don't remember. What is overflow?"

"It's when there's so much rain that the Gulf of Mexico rises. And the water flows into the city."

I'd never seen this much water before, but I didn't tell Henry that.

"When will it stop raining?" Henry asked.

"I'm sure it won't last long. By the time Mama and Papa are home, the storm will be over!" I said, trying to sound confident. I slid off the bed and pulled Henry with me. "Come on, let's play a game of checkers."

Henry seemed satisfied with that. He clapped his hands and followed me down the stairs. I set up the game on the kitchen table, and we played three games. I let Henry beat me once. He seemed to have forgotten about the storm and the rising water outside. But I hadn't. Each time the wind howled, a shiver snaked up my spine.

I wish Mama and Papa were home, I thought.

It was only mid-afternoon, but the house was dim. The storm outside seemed to have sucked up all the light.

I stood up to light the kerosene lamp and peeked out the window. The water was still gushing down the street. And then I saw something else that made me stiffen with fright.

A man, a woman, and a child were making their way through the water. The little girl was clutching a doll and a pillow. The mother and father had piles of belongings heaped onto their backs. The father was carrying a large framed photograph, struggling to keep hold of it in the wind.

Where are they going? I wondered. *Why would they leave their house?*

As they passed, I saw another group of people behind them, also hauling belongings. Then it hit me. They must be coming from lower ground, carrying whatever they could with them.

I swallowed the doom rising in my throat. If this many people were heading for higher ground, the storm must have been worse than I'd imagined.

I looked at Henry, who was moving checkers around the board, not paying any attention to me. I didn't know what to do.

Should I take Henry to higher ground too? But where? I thought quickly. We could follow the line of people and go wherever they were heading. Or go to Betsy's. She only lived a few blocks away.

But what if she's not there? I thought. *We'll be all alone.*

As I watched, a shrieking gust of wind slammed into the line of people. One man lost his balance. The trunk he was carrying flew from his grasp and opened, launching clothes and papers into the sky like confetti. The man lunged for the trunk but slipped and landed face-first in the water. I watched as he struggled to his feet against the driving wind.

My heart was a wild thing in my chest. *If a grown man can barely make it, there's no way*

Henry and I can, I realized. We couldn't go out in the storm, no matter what.

I slid the curtain shut. I couldn't bear to see any more. And I didn't want Henry to see it either. *Our house is solid,* I told myself. *We're better off inside.*

I wondered suddenly if my parents were OK. And Betsy and Anna. Surely they were all safe inside.

I ran to the telephone. Maybe I could call the Gilberts. I lifted the receiver, hoping to hear the operator's voice on the other end. But it was silent. The line was dead.

Henry appeared at my elbow, tugging my sleeve. "Who are you calling?"

"I wanted to talk to Papa. But the line is busy," I lied.

Another roar of wind slammed against the house, making my head ring. Henry's eyes filled with tears.

"Should we play another game of checkers?"
I asked.

Henry shook his head, tears rolling down his cheeks. "The storm is too loud," he whimpered.

I had to do something to distract him. I looked around, my eyes landing on the piano. Music might drown out the storm. "How about I play the piano?" I offered. Henry's legs weren't long enough for him to reach the pedals. "And you can sing."

I pulled Henry onto the piano bench beside me and played his favorite songs while he sang along. I punched the keys hard. The notes rang out as pellets of rain hit the window. I played faster.

"Play 'Row Your Boat' next!" Henry said.

I started to play the nursery rhyme, and we both sang, but then I stopped. I didn't want to think about boats, or streams, or water.

I switched to another tune instead. But as I dropped my foot onto the piano's pedal, I felt something wet. I looked down. The piano was standing in a puddle of water. The entire floor was wet, and the water seemed to rise as I watched. Water was seeping into the house, getting higher by the second.

I gulped. The storm was coming for us.

CHAPTER **FIVE**

The Mills's house
Saturday, September 8, 1900
5:00 p.m.

"Henry," I said, as calmly as possible. "We have to go upstairs."

He looked down at the water puddling, which he hadn't noticed until that moment, and let out a gigantic scream. I wrapped my arms around him to comfort him.

"Don't worry. We'll be safe upstairs," I promised. "The water won't get that high."

But even as I spoke, I felt a tinge of doubt. Would we be safe? Now that I was no longer playing the piano, the wind seemed louder than ever. It swirled around the house, battering the walls from all sides.

I lifted Henry from the piano bench and set him down on the wet floor. "What about the checkers board?" he asked. "Will it wash away?"

"We'll take it upstairs." I glanced around. "And your toy truck too."

I thought about what else we could save. Mama's rugs were already drenched and ruined. I remembered the man carrying the framed photograph. Mama would want her photographs saved. I grabbed them from the fireplace mantle.

Maybe her china and dishes too? I thought. But they were safe in the cupboard. The water couldn't possibly rise all the way to the cupboards, could it?

My feet squished in my soggy shoes as I gathered up everything I could carry in my arms. Henry stood at the foot of the stairs, watching me with round eyes.

"Hurry," he said. "I'm scared."

"Don't be scared," I said cheerily. "This is exciting! We're saving the checkers board from the scary storm. Just think, when you're old, you can tell your friends all about it!"

When you're old. The phrase stuck in my mind. Would my brother and I both live to grow old? I realized Henry's survival depended on me. I had to make sure he was OK. I had to make sure we survived the storm. I had to.

Suddenly a loud crash sounded behind me, and the wall shook. Something had hit the side of the house.

I knew I should stay away from the windows, but I had to see. I pressed my face to the glass. Outside, roof tiles were hurtling through the air, battering the side of our house. Toys, books, and clothes swirled in the raging water. A doll circled in the wind, landing face-down with a splash.

I felt frozen, my tongue thick in my throat. Dolls. Books. Toys. People's belongings. Things that shouldn't be outside. A house must have collapsed. Or more than one.

"Get upstairs, Henry!" I said. When I turned from the window, he was still standing at the foot of the stairs, frozen. "Now!" I yelled as forcefully as I could.

He turned and scooted up the stairs, checkers sliding off the board and clattering to the steps as he ran. I raced toward the stairs.

Another crash, so terrible and fierce my ears rang, came from the dining room. This crash was different than the first one. This one was inside the house.

"What was that?" Henry yelled to me, clearly terrified.

I looked back. A chunk of plaster had fallen from the ceiling, right onto the piano bench.

The same bench Henry and I had been sitting on moments earlier.

I leapt up the steps. My breath surged in my chest. "Henry!" I called to my brother. We had to get to my room, across from the collapsing ceiling. I hoped it would be safest.

I bumped into Henry at the top of the stairs. He was just standing there, not moving, not crying, not making a sound. Checkers were scattered at his feet.

I grabbed my brother's arm and pulled him into my room, slamming the door behind us. I leaned against the door and slithered to the floor. Henry crumpled onto my lap, still not making a sound.

The violent wind screamed, louder and louder. The house rocked in its grasp. Debris slammed against the walls.

I didn't know what to do. Would the storm get worse as the night went on? Or better? I knew nothing about storms. I thought about Betsy, so smart. She was probably listening to the wind right now, determining if it was getting weaker or stronger.

Thinking about Betsy made me want to cry. I was supposed to be dressing up and doing my hair with her and Anna. Instead, we were caught in a terrible storm. But I couldn't cry. Not with Henry on my lap, shaking and scared.

And then I heard it. Silence. The wind was no longer screaming, not as loud anyway.

The storm is letting up, I thought. *The worst is over.*

I slid Henry off my lap and ran to the window. Usually I could see straight into the neighbors' house. But now I saw nothing. The house was gone. It was just a mound of rubble in the dark, angry water.

Wind blasted at the window. The storm was back. The silence had just been a lull.

I ran back to Henry and held him tight.

Downstairs, I heard a crash. And then another. And another.

Our house is next, I thought.

And then the floor dropped from under us.

CHAPTER SIX

I lost my grip on Henry as I slid along the tilting floor. A split second later my body slammed into the wall, and I braced myself against the doorframe. Henry's soft body bumped into mine.

"Hold tight to me," I commanded.

I tried to calm my mind and think about what was happening. The house must have collapsed on one side. I knew the rest would follow. I looked up and saw the beams of the underbelly of the roof. The ceiling was completely gone.

The storm screamed, louder and more ferocious than ever. The roof above us lifted off the house. Rain poured in, and then the roof slammed down. The wind tried to wrestle it free again.

"Carrie, what's happening?" Henry cried.

I hugged him closer. "I don't know," I admitted. "It's the storm. But we're together. Whatever happens, at least we're together."

"Don't leave me," he whimpered.

"I won't," I told him.

But I didn't know what to do. We didn't have much time. If—or when—the roof collapsed on us, we'd be killed. I couldn't believe it. The house that had always been our safe place and shelter was now going to kill us.

I didn't want to die. I didn't want Henry to die.

We had to get out of the house.

The house shuddered below us, and the floor tilted the other way. I held tight to the doorframe.

The roof banged open and closed again, sending a shower of tiles to the floor.

A large chunk of roof slammed to the floor near the window. The window shattered in an explosion of glass.

The roof! I thought suddenly. The roof wouldn't kill us. It would save us.

"Henry," I said. "We're going on an adventure, OK? You're going to ride piggyback on me. We're going to make our way to the window. And then we're going to jump out."

"Jump?" Henry's voice was tight with fear.

"If we get separated," I went on, "hold on to anything that floats. Whatever you do, don't let go. OK? And I won't let go of you."

I felt Henry nod.

I hauled my little brother onto my back. He wrapped his legs and arms around me. And then I started to crawl toward the window.

I tried to hurry, but it was hard to move. Henry was heavy, and the wood floor was slick. Any minute now, it could collapse and swallow us up. But I had to keep going. Our lives depended on it.

One inch at a time, I told myself. I moved one crawl-step, then another. I tried not to think about the rain batting against us through the window. I tried not to think about the raging water waiting for us outside. I tried not to think about what might happen if I lost Henry.

I tried not to think at all.

At last we reached the window. I looked out to see that the water was only a few feet below us.

Now all I needed to do was shove the slab of roof out the open window. Then we'd jump onto it. The roof would be our raft in the swirling water.

Can I do it? Am I strong enough with Henry on my back?

I had to try.

I lodged my feet against the wall and curled my fingers around the piece of roof. Then I pushed. My muscles screamed. I pushed and pushed some more. At last, the piece of roof slid out the window and landed in the water below with a splash.

I crouched below the shattered window. "Crawl onto the windowsill," I told Henry. "Hurry!"

He grabbed the windowsill and climbed on. I squeezed beside him and clasped his hand. "We're going to jump. Whatever you do, don't let go of my hand. Ready? One . . . two . . . three!"

And then we leapt into the air, just as the house crashed apart behind us.

CHAPTER **SEVEN**

Henry and I landed on the piece of roof, hands still clasped. Debris was flying everywhere, and I shielded my brother's head with my arms.

The raft dipped and lurched in the water. It was small, about the size of a door, and I could only hope it would be able to keep us both afloat.

Our house and everything in it was gone. Henry's toys, all my dolls, Mama's pretty dresses . . . all of it had been washed away.

I thought about how I'd tried to save Mama's things. That seemed like a lifetime ago. Now I was just trying to save Henry and myself. None of our possessions mattered anymore.

The raft moved quickly through the swirling water. Rain pummeled us. I looked around, peering through the pouring rain. A flash of lightning lit up our surroundings, and I realized I didn't know where we were anymore. Galveston was no longer a city. Instead, it was a flooded, ruined wreckage.

The water tugged at our raft, sending us backward and forward. Would we be swept out into the Gulf? Our little raft would never survive in the ocean. I closed my eyes, holding Henry closer.

And then I heard the screams. We weren't the only ones out here.

"Help!" someone yelled.

"Save me!" called another voice.

I opened my eyes. Through the rage of the storm I could see shapes in the water. A panicked horse swam past, kicking and neighing. A woman's head surfaced. She screamed and was pulled underwater again.

My heart split into a million pieces. I couldn't help anyone, let alone save them. I couldn't do anything except cling to Henry and the raft.

Henry let out a small sound. At first I thought it was a whimper. Then I realized he was singing.

"Row, row, row your boat," he half-sang, half-sobbed.

"Gently down the stream," I joined in. We sang, louder and louder, drowning out the sounds around us as our makeshift raft was tossed about.

Suddenly, through the rain, I spotted something up ahead. A large, dark tree loomed. Our raft was headed straight for it at breakneck speed. If we hit it hard enough, our raft could splinter. We'd be doomed.

But maybe, just maybe, I thought, *I can grab onto a tree branch. The tree might hold us.*

I scooted forward to the edge of the raft. I would only have one chance. I clutched the bottom of the raft with one hand and held the other out in front of me.

"Hold on to the raft, Henry!" I cried. Then I braced for impact.

BAM! The raft slammed into the tree.

I curled my arm around a low-hanging branch, stopping the raft's momentum. But I couldn't hang on for long. I had to come up with another plan.

I peered around the tree. Another tree stood close by. Maybe I could swivel the raft around and lodge it between the two trees. It was our best chance.

I wrapped both arms around the tree branch, lifted my feet off the raft, and shoved the raft with my foot. A brilliant bolt of lightning illuminated Henry's wide, scared eyes as the raft shifted. I gave the raft another kick, and it butted up against the

tree. One more nudge. The raft didn't move. It was secure between the two trees.

I dropped onto the raft. We were safe for now.

Unless the water kept rising.

I tried to ignore the thought and turned to Henry. "We're safe here," I told him. "Should we play riddles?"

Henry didn't answer. His eyes were locked on something over my shoulder.

I turned to see a large, dark shape bobbing in the water. It looked like a ship with a lighted mast, sailing through the city. Then I realized it was an entire house, ripped clear off its foundation. Lamps were still burning in the upstairs windows. A face appeared in one of the windows, looking out.

The house floated out of sight, pushed by the driving wind. I knew it was only a matter of time until the house collapsed. I tried not to think about what would happen to the people inside.

"Let's play riddles," I said again, trying to sound strong.

I had to distract Henry from the horrors around us. Riddles was Henry's favorite game to play whenever we traveled to Houston on the train or went on a carriage ride.

"I'm flat as a leaf, round as a ring. I have two eyes, but I can't see a thing. What am I?" I asked.

Henry didn't answer. He just stared into the water.

"A button!" I said.

Henry didn't seem to hear me.

I started to worry. Henry was always happy and ready to play. Now he seemed just a shell of himself.

Even if we survive this storm, will Henry ever be himself again? I wondered. *Will I?*

The trees provided some shelter from the storm, but not enough. At any moment a roof tile spinning through the air could smash our heads. I knew we needed more protection. I grabbed what I could of debris that floated past, propping boards and pieces of plaster onto the raft to act as a shield against the wind.

I scooped a large bowl from the water and held it out to Henry. "Here's a hat," I said. He looked at me but didn't make a move. "Hold it over your head for protection," I told him.

Henry did as he was told but didn't say a word.

Time ticked by. I was so wet and so cold. Colder than I'd ever been in my life. I held onto Henry, hoping we could keep each other warm. Instead we shivered together as wind battered our makeshift shelter.

Then Henry lifted his arm and pointed.

Just a few feet away, a hand stuck out of the water. Then the face of a young black boy emerged. "Help me!" he cried before the water swallowed him up again.

I gasped. The boy was so close to us. I had to help him.

"Carrie! Do something!" Henry begged.

I stretched out my arm, trying to grab the boy's hand. But I couldn't reach him.

Just a little farther, I thought. I leaned over, straining to reach.

Our fingers touched. The boy's hand curled around mine. But our hands were slick with rain, and his fingers slipped from my grasp. Before I could take another breath, I toppled off the raft and plunged into the water.

CHAPTER EIGHT

Water closed over my head. Everything was so dark, so quiet. My sodden, heavy dress dragged me down, down, down. Time stood still.

"Carrie! Carrie!" Henry's voice broke through the silence.

I kicked my legs and splashed to the surface. "Henry!" I called. "I'm here!"

The whirling water tugged at me, and I kicked again. This time I kicked something soft. Whatever it was kicked back.

The boy! I realized.

I swiveled and grabbed his arm. Together we strained toward the slab of roof I'd wedged between the trees. I grasped the side of the raft. Henry reached his hand toward me.

"No!" I commanded. "Just hang onto the raft, or you might fall in."

Henry immediately dropped his hand. Even in the dark, swirling storm, I could see the fear on his face.

A wave washed over me, filling my mouth with gritty water. My feet touched a tree trunk, and I wrapped my legs around its trunk. Beside me the boy floundered, and I gripped his arm tighter.

"Crawl on!" I shouted to him. "I've got hold of the tree."

"No! You first," the boy said.

I didn't listen to him. Instead, I yanked his arm with all my might and pushed him onto the raft. He gasped and pumped his legs, then swung his legs onto the raft.

Another wave surged over me, but I held tight to the raft. I loosened one leg from the tree and bent my knee, then slammed my foot into the tree. My body catapulted onto the raft. I slithered on its wet surface. The boy grabbed my arms and pulled.

I was free of the water. And Henry was still safe.

Maybe we would survive after all.

As soon as I was fully settled, Henry crawled onto my lap. "I thought you'd be drownded!" he sobbed.

"I'm still here," I comforted him, smoothing his hair.

A flash of lightning blazed, illuminating the boy I'd pulled from the water. He looked to be about my age. "Thank you for helping me," he said.

I had to strain to hear his words over the raging storm around us. "We helped each other," I said, leaning closer. "I'm Carrie, and this is my brother, Henry."

"I'm William," the boy said.

Henry turned his head to look at William. "Hi," he said shyly.

"Hi, Henry," William said. "I have a brother about your age." His voice fell, and he lowered his head again. I didn't want to ask where his brother was.

After a moment, William raised his head again and went on. "My brother likes to play jacks. What's your favorite game?"

"Used to be checkers," Henry said. "But not anymore. I hate checkers!" He slammed his head into me and buried his face in my chest.

"We were playing checkers when the storm hit," I explained to William. I nudged Henry. "Tell him your second-favorite game. The one we play on train rides."

"Riddles," said Henry. He looked at William. "Do you know any?"

"Sure," said William. "I have a face but no eyes. Hands but no arms. What am I?"

Henry thought for a moment. "A clock?" he guessed.

"You're right!" William said.

Henry giggled. The sound of his laughter filled me with relief. I thought I might never hear Henry laugh again.

"Tell me another!" Henry squealed.

William told another and another as the rain pounded around us, softening as the night went on. The wind heaved dying breaths. It seemed the storm might finally be ending.

At last Henry dropped off to sleep, nestled in my arms. I braved a question that had been on my mind for what seemed like hours. "Where is your family?" I asked William.

"I don't know," he replied. "We got separated in the storm."

"Us too," I said. "My parents went to a party this afternoon. Henry and I were home alone."

There was a long pause, and I didn't think William would go on, but then he took a deep breath and told me his story.

"My father owns a dry goods store on Sixteenth," he said. "We were working, our whole family. Saturday is our busiest day. Even the rain didn't keep the customers away. They kept coming and coming, fast as the rain. And then water started filling the store. Some people left. Others stayed to wait it out." William stopped and gave a hard little laugh. "Wait it out! As if it were just a regular storm."

"Nobody knew it would be so bad," I said, aiming to comfort him.

William went on. "We climbed on tables and chairs to keep out of the water. One of my brothers—the one Henry's age—thought it was fun to keep jumping from the chair to the water. Our dog, Pixie, kept running around in the water too."

William swallowed and was silent for a moment. "We all loved Pixie. Especially my little brothers and my little sister. The storm kept getting worse and worse. And then the wind slammed through the door, breaking it apart. Pixie, the little rascal, went swimming out the door. My siblings begged me to go after her. I thought it would be easy, you know? Scoop up Pixie and run back inside. But I didn't know that the street was a river. I got swept away."

"You're safe now," I said. "The storm is starting to fade."

William shook his head. "That's not the end," he said. "I got swept away, but I ended up snagged in a mass of debris that was lodged against a building. I could still see the store, though, through flashes of lightning. And then all of a sudden I couldn't see it anymore. It collapsed."

I gasped and reached for William's hand. I knew it wasn't ladylike for a girl to hold a boy's hand, but I didn't care. None of that mattered anymore.

We sat in silence for a long time after that. Then William pointed to the sky. "Look!" he said. "The moon!"

I looked up to see the moon staring down at us. The sky was clear. The storm had passed.

I thought about everyone I knew, everyone I loved. Anna, Betsy, Mama, and Papa. I'd been so focused on keeping Henry alive that I'd pushed away nearly all thoughts of them during the night. Were they looking at the moon too? Had they even survived?

The thought of them pierced my heart. *Where are my parents? How will I ever find them in the wreckage of the city?*

CHAPTER **NINE**

Galveston, Texas
Sunday, September 9, 1900
6:00 a.m.

The sun rose, like it did every day. But today was different. Today the sun's light revealed death and destruction. From our perch on the raft, I could see the true damage the storm had brought.

Galveston was gone. Nothing was left.

I looked up and down the street. Only one house remained standing, leaning sideways. Stacks of timber, roof tiles, and broken furniture lined the street. Downed trees lay everywhere, their roots like fingers reaching to the sky. Most of the water had receded, but puddles still stood, trapped by the debris.

Somehow, the trees that held our raft had stayed strong.

"I have to find my parents," I told William. He nodded as he gazed around at the wreckage surrounding us.

"You should look for your family too," I said. "Maybe they . . ."

I stopped. I wanted to give him hope, but it was hard to find it among the destruction.

I nudged Henry awake. I didn't want him to see what was left of our city, but we had to move.

Rubbing his eyes, Henry looked around and started to cry. I didn't tell him to stop. I wanted to cry too.

William hopped to the ground and helped Henry and me off the raft. My feet sank into the slimy mud.

I held Henry's hand tightly in mine as we picked our way through the rubble. A baby carriage lay upside down, its wheels spinning in the light wind. Broken dishes crunched under my feet.

I almost couldn't bear to look. Everything everyone owned had been scrambled together in the storm.

And the smell. The smell was the worst part. Wet and horrible and rotten.

We passed a huge pile of debris. A pair of boots stuck out from the bottom of the pile. And then I realized that the boots were attached to a pair of legs.

William moved to the other side of Henry, and we kept him between us as we walked, trying to shield him from the horror around us. I couldn't look. I couldn't think. I just had to keep moving forward.

It was hard to tell where we were. All the landmarks I used to recognize around the city were gone. It seemed as if we were the only ones alive out here.

And then I heard them again. Cries for help.

People were trapped under collapsed buildings, I realized. Waiting to be rescued.

I swallowed my tears.

"There's nothing we can do," William said, sensing my distress. "We're just kids. We're not strong enough."

"But . . . we could try," I said. I looked around, but there was no telling where the cries were coming from.

"Look!" William said, pointing.

Up ahead, I spotted a group of men digging through the rubble, looking for survivors. I felt so relieved to finally see other people, I could have cried.

"They'll save them," William said.

We exchanged a look, and I knew we both recognized that not everyone could be saved.

"At least some of them," he added.

I hurried over to one of the men digging. "Please, sir!" I said. "Which way is Broadway?"

The man stopped what he was doing and pointed. Then he looked at William and scowled. I knew why right away. It was because William was black, and I was white.

I couldn't believe it. After everything that had happened, people still looked at skin color.

"Come on," I said to William, turning in the direction the man had pointed.

"I have to go the other way," William said. "To find my family."

I nodded. After spending all night clinging to the raft together, I wasn't ready for William to leave. I knew I might never see him again. But I also knew

I would always consider him a friend, no matter what.

I hugged him tightly. "I wish you luck," I said into his ear.

William hugged me back, then knelt and hugged Henry. "Remember those riddles, little man. You can tell them to your friends."

"Goodbye, William," Henry said in reply. "I love you."

William and I grinned at Henry's words. Henry didn't see our differences. He just saw another person who was like us—a survivor.

William gave us a final wave and turned away. Henry and I hurried toward Broadway. Toward the Gilbert mansion.

Broadway hadn't escaped the flood, even though it was on higher ground than the rest of the city. Timbers and shattered windows covered the street.

As we walked toward the Gilbert mansion, my throat felt thick. Had the mansion survived? Had my parents?

My heart leaped with relief when I saw the tall, brick mansion still standing on the corner. I raced up the steps and pounded on the door.

No one answered. Nothing moved inside. The house was deserted.

"Where is everyone?" Henry asked me very quietly.

Before I could answer, a man's voice called from the street. "You looking for someone? Try the courthouse." He pointed down the street. "Survivors are gathering there, looking for their loved ones." He wiped his brow, and I could see the sorrow on his face. I knew he'd lost someone.

"Thank you," I said.

Henry and I made our way toward the county courthouse on Twentieth Street, following the other survivors headed that direction. I kept Henry close as we walked, telling him riddles to distract him from the destruction around us.

Will my parents be at the courthouse? I wondered. *Will Betsy?* I tried to imagine all of us together again, and tears stung my eyes.

Inside the courthouse, hundreds of people milled about, not speaking, looking shocked.

"Mama!" Henry screamed. "Where are you?"

We pushed through the crowds of people. I scanned every face. My hope withered. None of the faces were Mama's or Papa's.

And then I saw her. Mama. She was huddled on the floor, head in her hands. Her blue dress, the one I had helped her choose so carefully, was now stained a muddy brown. But she was alive.

Henry raced over and threw himself at her. My mother's shocked, tear-stained face stared up at me.

"It . . . it can't be!" she croaked. "My loves! Is it really you?"

I collapsed next to her, hugging her close.

"But our house . . . ," Mama said, still in disbelief. "We tried to go find you. The house . . . it was gone. How did you survive?"

"Carrie saved us!" Henry said. "We jumped on the roof. And ended up in a tree."

Mama stroked my hair. "My smart girl."

I swallowed. I could hardly bring myself to ask. "Where's Papa?" I whispered.

"He's OK," Mama said. "He's helping with the rescue."

I closed my eyes, my mind reeling. We were lucky. So lucky. Our whole family had lived. I knew not everyone could say the same.

I hugged Mama and lay my head on her shoulder. My mind spun. We were together, but would anything be the same again? It seemed a lifetime ago that Betsy and I had walked home from school in the heat, talking about hair and clothes.

Suddenly I sat up straight. "Mama, I need to look for Betsy," I told her. My mother had said our house was gone, and Betsy only lived a few blocks away. Surely she'd gotten out and come to the courthouse too.

Mama didn't seem to want to let me go, but she nodded. "Don't be gone long," she said.

I made my way through the throngs of people in the courthouse. Not a sign of Betsy. *I can't give up hope,* I told myself. *She could be somewhere. She's probably with Anna and their parents.*

As I was making my way back to my mother, I heard my name. "Carrie? Carrie Mills?"

I turned to see Miss Stapleton, holding out her arms. I rushed over and hugged her tightly.

"I've been searching for my students," Miss Stapleton told me. "I'm so glad I found you."

"Have you found anyone else?" I asked. "What about Betsy? Have you seen Betsy?"

Miss Stapleton's face fell. She shook her head and touched my shoulder. "I'm so sorry, Carrie. I went to Betsy's home. The house collapsed. Betsy and her family are gone."

CHAPTER TEN

My chest tightened, and I gasped for air.
Betsy. Smart, ambitious Betsy. Gone. And Anna?
Beautiful, vivacious Anna. Gone too.

No. I wouldn't believe it.

I gasped again, and this time tears followed.
I covered my face and sobbed, my first tears since
the storm. It felt as if the tears would never end.

I remembered Betsy's words, just two days
ago, when I'd almost been hit by a carriage as we
walked home. *What would I do without my best
friend?* she'd said.

Now her words echoed eerily in my head. What would I do without her?

Suddenly it hit me. If it hadn't been for my parents' party, I would have been at Betsy's house last night.

If I'd spent the night as I'd planned, maybe it would have made a difference. Maybe I would have been able to save Betsy and Anna. Or maybe I would have been killed too. I'd been close to death so many times during the storm. But here I was, still alive. It wasn't fair.

"How can it be?" I asked Miss Stapleton, suddenly furious. "Betsy was so smart. She could have done anything with her life. Why her? Why Anna?"

Miss Stapleton shook her head. Her eyes were glazed with tears. "I don't know," she said. "But I do know that Betsy would want you to be happy, to do something with your life. She wasn't the only smart one."

"I'm not smart," I argued.

"How did you get through the storm?" Miss Stapleton asked.

I was surprised by her sudden question, but I told her quickly what had happened.

Miss Stapleton nodded when I was finished. "Without your quick thinking, your brother wouldn't be here," she said.

Maybe she was right. I'd done everything I could to keep Henry safe. I thought of William too. Where would he be now if we hadn't found each other?

Miss Stapleton watched my face. "Do you see now?" she said. "You can do anything. Follow your dreams. Follow your passions."

"I have no dreams," I said. "Not anymore. I used to care about fashion." I looked down at my ripped, dirty dress and snorted. "So silly. Clothes don't matter. Nothing I do will ever matter again."

"That's not true," she said. "Your actions matter. Look at the difference you made in Henry's life. Your actions, no matter how large or small, can make a difference."

Miss Stapleton bid me goodbye and went to search for others. I returned to my mother and Henry. Mama took one look at my tear-stained face and knew what had happened. I didn't have to say a word.

"Oh, Carrie, I'm sorry," she said.

I curled up next to her and cried until the tears would no longer come. I was tired, so tired. My eyes closed, and I slept.

When I woke, my father was kneeling next to me, stroking my hair. "Papa!" I cried, hugging him. My tears fell again.

Papa looked older now. His face was lined with sorrow and regret. I didn't need to ask what he'd seen out there. I could see it in his eyes.

"I'm going to stay in Galveston and help," Papa told me. "But you, Henry, and your mother need to leave the city. As soon as possible."

I stared at him. "Leave?" I repeated. "How can we leave?"

"The railroad across the bay to Houston will be repaired soon," he said.

"That's not what I meant," I said. "I meant I'm not leaving. I'm staying in Galveston."

"There's nothing here for us," Papa said. He sighed. "We'll move to Houston. I'll find another job at another bank."

I shook my head firmly. "No. We're staying here." I glanced at Mama and Henry. "Galveston is our home. We'll help rebuild. Even if it's only a little at a time. Our actions matter. They matter a lot."

Papa looked at me. I stared back, unflinching. Then he gave a small nod.

We would stay. We would help build the city back up to what it once was, a shining jewel on an island in the Gulf.

Galveston, Texas
September 9–16, 1900

My family and I spent the night in the courthouse with hundreds of others. Black and white, old and young, rich and poor. We were all equal now. We had nothing in common, yet we had everything in common. We were all Galvestonians. We were all survivors—and we had all lost something.

Over the next few days, help arrived. The Red Cross set up tents for the homeless. Hundreds of white tents lined the beach. The "New York of the Southwest" was now the "White City on the Beach."

Mama, Papa, Henry, and I crowded into one tent. It was nothing like living in our big house, but for now it was home.

I was determined to help, so I did. I spent the days handing out donated clothing to survivors. Every time I placed a garment in someone's hands, their eyes filled with tears of gratitude. I thought about what Miss Stapleton had said—small actions can mean a lot.

I remembered too her words that I could do anything, that I should follow my passion. My passion was clothes. And I realized that even that could bring happiness and beauty to someone's life. Maybe I actually could become a designer when I grew up. Maybe my love of fashion wasn't so foolish after all.

Every night, before I went to sleep, I told Betsy about my day. She wasn't there to hear my words, but I knew she'd be proud of me.

One day, Henry and I were walking along the beach to our tent. Suddenly Henry took off at a gallop.

"Henry!" I screamed, feeling the old fear grip me. I ran after him. But then I saw whom he was running toward.

William.

Henry tackled William's legs, nearly knocking him off balance. William grinned down at Henry. A small, gray dog leapt around their feet, barking.

"Hello, William," I said. I felt shy, suddenly.

William tipped his hat and smiled. "Hello, Carrie."

I looked down at the dog. "Is this Pixie?"

William patted the dog's head and nodded. "Can you believe it? She made it through the storm. I was shocked when she ran up to me through the wreckage, barking and wagging her tail."

"Amazing," I said.

Henry tossed a stick, and Pixie ran after it. Henry threw another, giggling as Pixie jumped into the air and caught it in her mouth.

I looked at William. "And your family . . .?"

William's mouth tightened, and he shook his head. "My father survived," he said. He cleared his throat. "We are going to rebuild the store. Together."

"I convinced my parents to stay too," I told him.

"Good," he said. "This city is our home. Yours and mine."

I nodded, and we both turned to look out at the Gulf, serene and sparkling under the September sun.

"I'm not leaving," I agreed. "Not ever."

A NOTE FROM THE AUTHOR

In the late 1800s, Galveston, Texas, was a booming community. The city's location on an island in the Gulf of Mexico made it a prime spot for shipping and trading. At the time, it was the most important cotton-trading port in the world. But on September 8, 1900, the Great Galveston Hurricane—also called the Great Storm—swept over the city in what remains the deadliest natural disaster in U.S. history.

The hurricane that hit Galveston began off the coast of Africa in late August and raged over Cuba and the Florida Keys before striking Galveston in mid-afternoon on September 8. Wind speeds reached 135 miles per hour, making it a Category 4 hurricane on today's Saffir-Simpson scale.

The storm surge flooded the city with fifteen feet of water. More than 3,600 buildings and homes were destroyed. Most official reports state that at least eight thousand people died, but the number could be anywhere between six thousand and twelve thousand people.

On the morning of September 8, 1900, most Galveston residents had no idea how strong—or deadly—the storm would become. At the time, Galveston had a population of thirty-eight thousand people, most of whom had weathered many tropical storms before the hurricane.

Without modern weather satellites and computer technology, storms were hard to predict and track. U.S. weather officials hesitated to use words like *hurricane* or *cyclone* because they didn't want people to panic. (In fact, in 1891, Isaac Cline, chief meteorologist at Galveston's Weather Bureau, wrote that a strong hurricane could never make landfall in Galveston. He believed that the shallow, sandy water surrounding the island would slow a hurricane down.) As a result, many residents believed the coming storm was just like those they'd survived before.

The storm caused many ordinary people—just like you and me—to take extraordinary measures to save themselves and others. Survival stories, just like Carrie's, are part of the fabric of the storm. In my research, I found many accounts of courage, hope, and survival among the tragic tales. When the roof of St. Mary's Orphanage collapsed, three boys were thrown into the storm. They swam to an uprooted tree and clung to it for more than a day as it floated out to the Gulf, then back on shore.

In another miraculous story, sixteen-year-old Anna Delz was washed out to the Gulf by the storm before being swept back across the entire island to the mainland. She slept on a pile of lumber with no idea where she was. In the morning, after the water receded, she walked until she discovered that she was in the town of La Marque, Texas, where her aunt lived. Delz found her aunt's house and was later reunited with her Galveston family.

Strangers also helped each other survive. A man named Arnold Wolfram was huddling in a doorway when he saw a ten-year-old boy being sucked down a storm drain. Wolfram ran to the boy and pulled him out, then told the boy to tie his shoes to his head as protection from flying objects. The two were swept into the branches of a tree, where they huddled together and struggled through the storm.

The Great Galveston Hurricane (also known as the Great Storm of 1900), turned much of Texas's great city to rubble. Approximately ten thousand residents were left homeless after a fifteen-foot storm surge swept across the tiny barrier island, which sat less than nine feet above sea level.

Wreckage slammed into the tree, nearly uprooting it, but it also provided a bridge to a nearby house. The two made their way to the house, where they found shelter. After the hurricane, Wolfram and the boy became lifelong friends.

When I was preparing to write the book, these were the stories that stood out to me. I thought about the three orphan boys clinging to the tree and wondered what had gone through their minds during those long hours. I thought about Anna Delz, all alone, not knowing if she'd survive. I thought about the man risking his own safety to save a boy he didn't know. I knew there were countless other stories that had never been told, stories of bravery and heroism amidst the raging winds of the hurricane.

I wanted my main character, Carrie, to show such bravery. I wanted her to discover strength and smarts she didn't know she had. Carrie must figure out how to keep her brother safe, and she's willing to risk her own life to do so.

When the storm ended in the early hours of September 9, 1900, Galveston was almost completely destroyed. Those who had survived had no food or shelter. Immediately, city officials began organizing rescue teams. The Red Cross set up temporary shelters and tents for the homeless. Bodies were loaded onto carts to be buried at sea, because there was not enough room to bury them all on the island. Unfortunately, Gulf currents washed many bodies back onto shore. The only solution was to burn them. Funeral pyres set up along the beaches blazed night and day for several weeks.

In 1900 Galveston had a diverse population. White, black, and Hispanic men worked together on the city's wharf, loading and unloading ships. But despite its diversity, Galveston was racially segregated. African Americans had to ride in the back of trolleys and sit in separate sections in the theater. Black children went to separate schools from white children. Black citizens had to swim in a separate area on the beach.

But natural disasters, such as the Galveston Hurricane, have no boundaries based on race. The storm wiped out white and black neighborhoods alike. After the hurricane struck, people of all races and ethnicities worked side by side to save each other.

Daniel Ransom, an African American man, saved forty-five people from the roiling waves. He dove into the water and pulled people to safety in a nearby brick building. A white man named George Boschke opened his home to African Americans seeking shelter. At the Boschke home, white people and black people sang hymns together to drown their fears.

When I read about the ways in which African American and white residents came together to help each other, I knew I wanted to incorporate that into Carrie's story. I came up with the character of William, who is the same age as Carrie. Although they don't know each other, due to segregation, they don't see each other as different. They're both alike—both Galvestonians, both trying to survive, both worrying about their families. And, like Arnold Wolfram and the boy, they become lifelong friends.

Although Galveston was rebuilt, it never achieved its former glory as the "New York of the Southwest." Scared by the 1900 hurricane, many shipping and manufacturing businesses relocated to Houston's safer harbor.

But the Galveston Hurricane had some lasting positive effects on meteorology—the study of weather and weather forecasting. After the Great Storm, more efforts were put into hurricane studies and hurricane forecasting. Today the National Weather Service tracks storms and weather patterns around the clock, broadcasting warnings and watches so people can be prepared.

When I think about Galveston, I like to imagine Carrie, William, and Henry, standing on the beach, looking out at the Gulf, inspired to stay and rebuild their city. They have hope, strength, and determination—qualities that helped them survive the hurricane.

These qualities are not limited to race, gender, or age. I hope this story inspires you—no matter if you are a boy or a girl, no matter your race—to discover your own hidden strengths and face any challenges that come your way.

GLOSSARY

ambitious (am-BISH-uhs)—possessing a desire for success, honor, or power

barometer (buh-ROM-i-ter)—an instrument that measures air pressure and is used to forecast changes in the weather

chiffon (shi-FON)—a very thin fabric made of silk

debris (duh-BREE)—the junk or pieces left from something broken down or destroyed

ferocious (fuh-ROH-shuhs)—fierce or savage

hurricane (HUR-i-keyn)—a tropical cyclone with winds of 74 miles (119 kilometers) per hour or greater that is usually accompanied by rain, thunder, and lightning

knickers (NIK-erz)—loose-fitting, short pants gathered at the knee

makeshift (MEYK-shift)—serving as a temporary substitute

menacing (MEN-uh-sing)—dangerous or possibly harmful

momentum (moh-MEN-tuhm)—the force that a moving body has because of its weight and motion

nonchalant (non-shuh-LAHNT)—a relaxed manner, free from concern or excitement

ominous (OM-uh-nuhs)—considered a sign of evil or trouble to come

overflow (OH-ver-floh)—something that flows or fills a space and spreads beyond its limits

pompadour (POM-puh-dawr)—a woman's hairstyle in which the hair is brushed into a loose, full roll around the face

segregated (SEG-ri-gey-tid)—separated by race or ethnicity

streetcars (STREET-kahrs)—vehicles for carrying passengers that run on rails and operate mostly on city streets

swells (swelz)—long rolling waves, or series of waves, in the open sea

tapered (TEY-purd)—becoming gradually smaller at one end

vivacious (vi-VEY-shuhs)—full of energy and good spirits

MAKING CONNECTIONS

1. How would you describe the setting of the book? Does the setting change throughout the course of the story? How does the setting affect Carrie and Henry?

2. In Chapter Two, Carrie sees a group of African American kids on the far side of the beach. She says, "Even outside of our separate schools, black kids and white kids didn't mingle." Why do you think that is? Does that change by the end of the story?

3. At the end of the story, Carrie vows to stay in Galveston and help rebuild. In your own words, describe why she feels this way. What do you think her motivation is? Would you stay if you were in her position?

ABOUT THE AUTHOR

Jessica Gunderson grew up in the small town of Washburn, North Dakota. She has a bachelor's degree from the University of North Dakota and an MFA in Creative Writing from Minnesota State University, Mankato. She has written more than 75 books for young readers. Her book *President Lincoln's Killer and the America He Left Behind* won a 2018 Eureka! Nonfiction Children's Book Silver Award. She currently lives in Madison, Wisconsin, with her husband and three cats.